The Amish Muffin Murder

By
Ruth Bawell

Amish Mystery and Suspense

Table of Contents

The Mystery Begins...

Chapter 1

Summervale, Pennsylvania

"Katie, will you get that other teapot out to the porch? Our guest is waiting! But be quiet, he said he came here for quiet and to think."

"I will take the tea *Grossmammi,* and I will be quiet, but first I must take this to the guests in the sitting room."

"*Ach jah*! I'd almost forgotten. All right, then after you are done."

Katie nodded and carefully carried the tray of breakfast pastries into the bright, airy room. It was busier than usual this weekend and, though Katie was thankful for the guests to help pay for the mortgage on the farm where she and her grandmother lived, she was tired. Yet, at the same time she was itching for another mystery. It had been several months since her previous one wrapped up, and since then she'd found one lost cat, discovered a child hiding trinkets in the trunk of a tree, and solved the case of the missing shoes, which was hardly a case at all.

She set the tray down delicately, arranging it while the guests chatted about their plans that day. Standing, she stretched her back and walked back toward the kitchen. Her mind wandered toward her lack of mysteries lately. Was nothing mysterious in Summervale anymore?

Her stomach clenched with the fact that it wasn't just the mysteries that she missed—though they were a large part of it. She missed the handsome Detective Samuel Bradford. It was terrible of her, of course, and she had prayed that the Lord would take away her small crush on him. If only she could think of David like she'd used to.

Yet it was Samuel's face that she saw at night when she was saying her prayers before bed, and his face she woke up to with the wonder if some type of criminal activity would bring him back to Summervale. Of course it wouldn't, and that wasn't something she should hope for, yet a small part of her did.

Rearranging the next tray so that the teacups and teapot were balanced, she paused before heading to the back porch. She needed to be level headed about this. Samuel was a *detective*. He was not Amish. Just because he was handsome and shared her affinity for mystery did *not* mean that it was all right for her to fancy him. In fact, those were all reasons *not* to like him.

She pushed her shoulders back just as her grandmother bustled into the room. "*Lappich aedel*—you are such a silly girl. Didn't I tell you he needs his tea on the porch?"

"*Ya* and I'm taking it out now *Grossmammi*." Her grandmother could be so impatient at times, especially when guests were involved.

"Here, let me take it. You follow with the water and juice pitchers."

Katie obeyed, picking up the heavy ceramic pitchers to following her grandmother as she disappeared through the back door.

The next moment, the sound of breaking glass was accompanied with her grandmother's scream. Katie slammed the pitchers down on the side table and rushed out the back door, skidding to a halt at the image before her.

One of their guests was sprawled on the ground, and he looked dead.

***

Katie stood frozen, looking down at the man while her grandmother cried out, the contents of the tray shattered on the ground in front of her. Katie's keen eyes took in the surroundings. He was on the ground, face down, with his arms at his side like he'd fallen forward and not been able to help himself.

On the table next to where he'd been sitting sat a water glass and a partially eaten blueberry muffin.

"Katie!" her grandmother shouted. "*Do* something!"

She rushed forward, careful not to touch anything, and knelt down beside the man. Resting two fingers at his neck to feel for a pulse, her heart lurched when she felt nothing there. He was most certainly dead.

"I've just called 911," a woman said. She was one of their yearly guests, and stood with her cell phone in her hand, eyes wide.

They waited less than ten minutes before an ambulance came up to the door and men rushed through the house and to the man. They soon concluded what Katie had, that the poor man had passed away.

She overheard her grandmother talking with one man, explaining that the guest, Philip Julander, had specified that he had food allergies. She asked if it could be related to that. The medical assistant said it was possible, which eased her grandmother's worry some, if anyone's worries about death could be eased.

Soon the police arrived and began taking their statements, and Katie found her eyes searching the road for Samuel's detective car. She berated herself and focused on the kind woman asking her questions, though her mind wandered.

Had this been an accident?

There was no evidence to suggest foul play, except for the fact that a perfectly healthy, middle-aged man had just keeled over on their porch. *That* certainly wasn't normal. Then again, what would anyone have against him?

"Miss?" the woman said.

Katie blinked. "I'm sorry, what did you say?"

"I just told you to make sure you don't leave town until our investigation into the death is over."

"Of course not," Katie said with a forced smile. "Is there any reason to think this was anything other than a natural death?"

The woman blinked, obviously surprised by Katie's question. "Oh, please, miss, don't jump to conclusions. These types of things happen all the time. My guess would be aneurism or some type of existing physical issue, though don't quote me on that until the coroner does his exam. Don't worry yourself."

Katie wanted to laugh and tell the woman she certainly *wasn't* worried, but she kept that thought to herself. She couldn't be sure, but she had a gut feeling that this poor man's death was more—much more—than something that happened all the time.

Chapter 2

The unnatural silence of the guesthouse haunted her the next morning. Due to the uproar the day before, their guests had made other arrangements, leaving the house empty. Thankfully, none of the guests had been too upset, but Katie could tell her grandmother was unhappy at the loss of business. She was in her room still, despite the later hour of the morning, which left Katie to stew downstairs in the kitchen at her favorite reading nook.

A loud knocking echoed through the empty house and Katie jolted, nearly dropping her book. Who could it be?

Running her hands over her apron and making sure her bonnet was properly adjusted, she walked quickly through the house to the front door.

"Detective Bradford," she said with wide eyes when she opened the door.

He stood there, nearly filling the doorway, dressed in a suit and tie with dark sunglasses propped on his head, nestled his thick brown hair.

"*Gute mariye,*" he said. His greeting surprised her, but she responded in kind. "And remember, it's Samuel. May I come in? I have a few questions for you."

Sudden dread clenched at her stomach. He wasn't here to take her or her grandmother to the police station again, was he?

"Don't worry," he added quickly, as if seeing the fear on her face, "I can conduct all of my questions here."

She forced a small smile. "That's good to know." Stepping back, she allowed him to enter. The faint scent of strong soap left a masculine, musky scent in the air as he passed her, and she felt her cheeks heat at his nearness.

Stop this at once, Katie! She chastised herself.

"Would you like to sit?" She indicated a chair in the sitting room.

"Actually, could you show me where you found the body?" His eyes narrowed as if seeking out any hint of how she was fairing after finding a dead body on their back porch.

"Yes, this way." She turned around, ducking her head before his intense gaze could see more than she wanted him to—namely her reaction to his presence.

They walked through the house and out the back door. She stepped to the edge of the porch and then pointed with her finger. "We found him laying there, his arms at his side like he hadn't been able to stop himself from falling."

His gaze assessed her, then turned toward the area where the body had been. He circled around the area, tilting his head a few different ways, and then pulled out pictures from a file folder he'd carried under his arm. Holding them up, he judged the angles and moved around to see what the pictures showed.

"Why are you here?" she asked. The question sounded accusatory, but she was just curious. The woman had thought that the death was caused by natural causes, but if Detective Bradford was here, didn't that mean it *wasn't* natural?

After a long pause while he kept his gaze on the chair and side table, he turned toward her.

"The man was poisoned."

Her eyes widened, and he cocked an eyebrow.

"What?" she asked in his silence.

"Did you *know* that already?"

"No," she said quickly, wanting to make sure she didn't appear guilty. But she *had* had her suspicions. "But it seemed odd that he would just drop dead here." She felt goosebumps on her arms and wrapped them around herself. She may be an investigator by nature, but that didn't mean death was easy to take.

"True," he said, nodding slowly.

"Who was he?" she asked.

"A local businessman. A loan officer from the next town over. I was told he came to get away for a few days."

She knew that much already. "But *who* was he?" She wondered if he would understand what she was asking and, if he did, if he could answer her.

"That is the question of the day."

She frowned up at him, watching as a deep "v" crested his brow.

"What do *you* think happened?" he invited.

***

Katie was shocked that *he* was asking *her* what she thought! Did this mean he considered her a worthy detective? She had to rein in her thoughts and try to be objective. Looking down at the spot where the man had died, she narrowed her eyes as she remembered the scene in its entirety.

"As I already said, I saw that his arms were down, as if he hadn't even tried to stop his fall. But I also noticed that he had a muffin next to him. It was blueberry and there was about a third of it left."

"Is that strange? I mean, do you make the muffins for your guests?"

"We do," she agreed, "but *Grossmammi* said he apparently had allergies. Someone had arranged to have special food brought in to him."

"Someone?" Samuel leaned forward, as if this information was extremely important.

"Yes, I think it was from my friend Emma's bakery. That's the closest bakery in town."

He scribbled down notes furiously and then looked up at her. "He didn't request the muffin?"

She thought back, but shook her head. "I don't know. I think *Grossmami* took care of that."

"Could I speak with her?"

"She was resting when I checked last, but I could wake her up."

He frowned. "No, that's all right. I'm sure she needs rest after all of this. I can come back."

His simple words, promising to come back, made Katie happier than she could say, but she schooled her features. "Can I help you with anything else?"

He shook his head no. "I don't think so. *Denki.*"

There it was—the Pennsylvania Dutch phrase rolled off his tongue like it was his maiden tongue. How was that possible?

"What?" he asked, looking up at her.

"Pardon me if this is rude, but how is it that you know words like *denki* and *gute mariye*?" The minute she asked, she felt foolish. Maybe he had grown up in the area and had friends who taught him the language. Or maybe…well, she didn't know how else, but she shouldn't have asked.

"I used to be part of the Amish community."

Her eyes bulged. "You did?"

He nodded, looking slightly uncomfortable. "Yes, but I've got to be going. Thank you for your help."

Katie wanted to ask him so many questions. Why had he left the community? Did he miss it? Would he tell her when he found something about the case?

Instead, she watched him leave, his tall form folding into the front seat of the car. It was strange, thinking of him as being part of her community at one point. Who were his parents?

The questions were endless, but she couldn't spend her energy thinking about them. Instead she needed to focus her attention on the case at hand. Of course she wasn't *formally* invited to take part in it, but Samuel *had* asked her for her input. It made her feel warm inside knowing that he valued what she would say about the case.

A smile overtook her features as she thought about them working yet another case together.

If only a man hadn't lost his life. Who was the man? Did he have enemies? Why would someone choose to hurt him? How had they done it? Thinking back, she wished she would have looked more closely at the muffin she'd seen, but the police wouldn't have let her even if she'd tried.

Sighing, she went back to her reading nook. Tomorrow she planned on doing some digging at the library on who their guest was. Until then, she'd lose herself in the pages of a mystery.

Chapter 3

Katie pulled on a light sweater as she prepared to go into the library to research Philip Julander. A knock sounded at the door, and her heart leapt. Was it Samuel?

When she opened the door, she couldn't help but feel the sting of disappointment, which she quickly tried to ignore. It was David, looking wild-eyed and handsome.

"*Gute mariye*, Katie."

"*Gute mariye*, David." She ducked her head in welcome and asked if he wanted to come in. When he refused, she noted how his foot tapped in impatience. "What is it?" she asked.

"It's Emma—the bakery," he quickly corrected. "They are shut down and there are police everywhere, going in and out and even searching through their trash. I'm worried about them."

Katie could imagine the scene well, knowing that their house had looked the same just two days before.

"Oh no." The realization struck her like a lightning bolt. She had told Samuel about the muffin and that it was from the bakery in town—Emma's bakery. Had she brought this upon them? But she had only told the truth from what she had observed. Was she supposed to keep that information secret?

That had happened on the last case, and things would have been cleared up more quickly had she simply been open about what she knew.

"You need to come," David said, breaking into her thoughts. "Emma will want to see you."

Katie *wanted* to go, but now she felt guilty. Still, Emma would need her friends with her. "Let's go," she agreed.

"I've brought my buggy. Come on."

They rode into town at a quick clip, and soon David had pulled his buggy up near the bakery. He had accurately described the scene to her. Police cars were lining the street, some with flashing lights, and there was a perimeter established with more of the yellow tape and officers to enforce it. Not that anyone was drawing near. Most folks were trying their best to steer clear of the activity.

The only people close were tourists who thought the whole thing a spectacle. *Of course*, Katie thought.

They walked up to the edge of the activity, where Emma and her father, Atlee Bender, stood with an officer.

"Emma," Katie called out as they drew near.

The officer turned around, a scowl on his face. "This area is restricted."

"Please," Emma said, stepping forward, "may I speak with them? They are my friends."

The officer regarded Emma, then Katie and David, and finally nodded his head once. "All right, but no one goes inside."

Katie and David both shook their heads "no" in agreement and slid under the tape, but only as far as where Emma and her father stood.

"What's happened?" Katie asked, though she had a feeling she knew *exactly* what was going on.

"We do not know," Atlee said, his hand stroking his beard in a nervous way. "They came in and swarmed the bakery like ants, and now here we are, removed from our own business." He shook his head, a look of frustration and sadness on his face.

Katie frowned, knowing that she had been the reason anyone came in the first place. She was about to say something when she spotted Detective Samuel. Her pulse picked up speed and she felt a delicate blush tint her cheeks. This was foolishness.

But maybe she could find out something from him—if she could catch his attention.

"Katie?" Emma said. Katie turned away from where she'd seen Samuel and met her friend's eyes. "Do you know anything about this?"

Opening her mouth to reply, Katie was caught off guard when she heard her name.

"Katie?"

She turned around, and came face to face with Samuel.

***

Saved from having to respond to her friend in the moment, Katie now found herself alone with Samuel, Emma and David's looks like daggers across from them. Didn't they understand that this was her chance? She was talking with a *real* detective about a *real* case!

She felt bad knowing that Emma was involved in the way she was, but everything Katie was doing was for her friend. To prove that they had no part in what was going on.

"What are you doing here?" Samuel asked.

She wasn't sure when she'd started thinking of him as Samuel instead of Detective Bradford, but she had. Though whether or not she would call him that, she hadn't decided yet.

"David told me about the police here, and I came down to see how my friend Emma was doing. Was … was this my fault?"

He frowned down at her. "Your fault? What do you mean?"

"I told you about the muffin and how it was from the bakery. It's my friend Emma's family's bakery and I would hate to think that I brought this on them." Telling Samuel this, she realized how guilty she felt. Tears sprung to her eyes, and though she was not one to cry, she felt the desire to do so now.

Samuel noticed as well and softened his gaze toward her. "It's not your fault at all Katie."

"But I—"

"We found another body," he blurted, and then slammed his mouth shut as if he shouldn't have said anything.

Her eyes grew round. "Really?"

"I shouldn't have said anything."

"Who was it?"

He glanced around, as if to see who was near them, then leaned closer to her. "It was another loan officer."

"Same as Mr. Julander?"

He nodded.

Her mind whirled with possibilities. Who would target loan officers? And why?

"But ..." she glanced back at Emma who was now in conversation with David. He rested his hand lightly on her arm for a moment, and then yanked it away as if realizing what he was doing. "What's the connection to the bakery?"

"We found another blueberry muffin there."

Katie gasped. He couldn't think that Emma or her father had anything to do with the murders, did he?

"You don't think—"

"I haven't come to any conclusions yet, Katie. Believe me, I'm not one to jump to suspicion. I prefer the detecting process."

Of course he did. He was a detective. Katie chided herself for thinking that he would suspect someone without evidence. Though the reality that there were poisonous muffins coming from the shop begged the question of *how* they'd come from the shop. The poison had to have been put in after.

"I don't understand," she said, reasoning through the evidence so far. "There can't be a connection between the Benders and these loan officers. Can there?"

"That's what I hope to find out." He looked serious, his gaze intent on her. "Do *you* know of any connection?"

"No," she said immediately, shaking her head to add emphasis. Atlee Bender and his daughter Emma were two of the best people she knew. Kind, gracious, giving— they would never let a family go hungry if a loaf of bread could help the situation.

"I didn't think so," he said, a half-smile on his lips, "But I had to ask."

"Where will you go next?"

"Ah, you can hardly expect me to give away my detecting secrets, can you?"

She flushed at his joking but couldn't help her smile. "I suppose not."

He grew serious then. "You'll be careful, won't you Katie?"

"What do you mean?" she asked.

"I have a feeling you won't leave this case alone, but whoever is behind his is dangerous—obviously. I don't want …" he pursed his lips, looking away as if to compose his thoughts before he looked back at her. "Just be careful."

His sudden interest in her wellbeing made her feel breathless and excited at the same time. "I will."

"Katie we need to go," David said. He stood right behind her, making her jump at his closeness.

"I'm almost done." She gave him a look and he glanced between her and Samuel.

"Fine." He left her with Samuel, and when she looked back, she saw an odd expression on his face.

"Are you his *aldi?*"

She felt her blush return at his question. "No!" Her response was so immediate he looked shocked. "Um, that is, no I'm not his girlfriend."

He looked relieved, or maybe she was imagining it. But either way, she knew she needed to escape his gaze and the intensity of his deep blue eyes.

"I should go."

"*Gute nochmidawk,* Kaite," Samuel said with a smile.

"*Gute nochmidawk,* Samuel." The minute she said his name, she realized her mistake—she betrayed her thoughts of him with the familiarity with which she addressed him. Nodding once, she turned and hurried away, feeling his eyes on her.

She had to stop this infatuation with a man she could never care for. She'd focus on the case instead of the handsome detective, if she could separate the two.

Chapter 4

The next day, David showed up at the guesthouse again. Though he'd appeared slightly affronted that she had sent him away while she talked with Samuel, he seemed back in good spirits this morning.

"Are you ready?"

"I am," she said, climbing into the buggy beside him.

They had deiced that they would go and talk with the loan officer the next town over. After her talk with Samuel, Katie had gone to the library as planned and discovered where Philip Julander worked from an article in the newspaper a few years back. The sun shone brightly around them, and Katie anticipated the visit with anxious excitement. She loved investigating, and today it actually felt as if she was doing something.

"What were you and that detective talking about yesterday?"

She tried to gauge David's mood and the source of his question. Why did it matter? He knew she was investigating the case. "He was explaining what was going on at the bakery."

"But isn't he not supposed to share those things? That can't be all right with the people he works for."

She had thought of this, but she also assumed that if Samuel was telling her something, he'd already considered the risk and decided it was all right to share. He trusted her, she could see that much in his eyes, but how did she explain that to David without bringing up more questions about *why* he would trust her.

"I'm sure that he didn't share something he couldn't with me." At least she hoped not.

"I don't think that you should talk to him so much."

Now she turned to look at him, shocked. "Why would you say that? I'm trying to solve this case to prove that Emma and her father had nothing to do with poor Mr. Julander's death. Sa—Detective Bradford is the best lead I have in order to do that!"

David's brow was furrowed, and she couldn't tell if he'd noticed her slipup of using Samuel's name or not.

"I just don't think it's wise."

He wouldn't look at her or give her a reason why, so she slipped into the comfort of her own thoughts and let the silence rest around them.

When they pulled up in front of the loan office, there was one car out front. She hoped that one of the workers would be there for them to talk to, or else they would have wasted a trip.

Thankfully the front door opened, and once her eyes had adjusted to the dimness, she saw that a man sat behind a desk. He looked startled when they entered, but then steadied his face.

"How can I help you? Are you two interested in a loan?"

Katie blushed. The man thought that she and David were a couple. Of course it was a completely natural guess, but it made her stomach clench in a strange, not pleasant way. How had her feelings toward David changed so much so quickly? An image of Samuel, unbidden, popped into her mind and she shoved it away.

"Hello, my name is Katie and this is David. We have a few questions for you about Mr. Julander."

The man opened his mouth, and then closed it again, looking confused. "Philip?"

"Yes," she said, boldly stepping forward.

"Well, um, I guess … please, have a seat."

They sat and she began her questions, asking about Philip and his past working for the company. He seemed to be very affected by his coworkers' deaths. At one point he answered a question and gestured so broadly that he sent a mug of coffee toppling over the desk.

"Oh!" he cried out, shaking his head. "And this is why I don't drink coffee. Excuse me while I get something to clean this up." He rushed toward the back of the office and disappeared.

"He looks very distraught."

"He does," Katie agreed.

Keeping an eye on the door Ralph had exited through, she stood up and peered over his desk. She saw a handwritten list, the corner just peering out under a manila file folder.

Careful not to touch the paper, she edged a portion of it away with her knuckle.

"What are you doing?" David said in a loud whisper.

Her eyes bulged when she saw Atlee Bender's name written at the top. Risking another glance at the door, she moved to step around the desk, noting the other names on the list as she did so. But in her haste, she tripped over David's foot and tumbled into the desk that sat behind Ralph's, her knocking a cup of pens and pencils to the floor.

Mad at herself, she rushed around the desk to pick them up before Ralph got back. Her hands reached under the desk for the last pencil when it rested on something else instead. Frowning, she pulled it out. It was a small plastic baggie that contained some sort of seeds. They reminded her of something.

Without thinking, she opened the bag and poured a few of the seeds into a tissue she grabbed from off the desk. She folded the tissue over the seeds and shoved it into the pocket of her dress. Then she righted the pens and pencils and hopped back to her seat just as the sound of Ralph's footsteps came their way.

"I'm sorry," he said, sniffing and rubbing his red eyes. "I'm going to have to ask you to leave. I—I'm not feeling very well."

Strange, Katie thought. He didn't look terribly ill, merely a little blotchy as if he'd rubbed his eyes too much.

"We thank you for your time, and we're sorry for you loss," David said.

Ralph followed them to the door, and Katie felt, rather than saw, his eyes on them as they left. There was something going on in that office, and Katie was going to get to the bottom of it.

***

David drove Katie to the library and she hopped out, thanking him for the ride but happy to be out of his sullen silence. He had been acting strangely, and she wasn't sure what to make of it. But now she saw Emma, her chin resting thoughtfully—if not a little sad looking—on her fist.

"Hello Em," she said, sitting down across from her friend.

Emma didn't reply, and merely looked at her, the remnants of tears still in her eyes.

"What's wrong?" Katie asked.

"What's *not* wrong? The bakery is closed, the police think my *Daed* or I had something to do with the murders, my *Mamm* is beside herself with sadness. It's *baremlich.*"

It *was* terrible, Katie thought, but she had things she had to discuss with Emma if she was going to solve this case and prove the Bender's innocence.

"Emma, have you seen these seeds before?" She pulled the tissue from her pocket and opened it carefully so as not to spill the seeds.

"No," Emma frowned, "but I could look them up if you want. Where did you get these?"

"We went to visit the loan office where the two victims worked."

"*Victims?*" Emma repeated.

Katie couldn't think of a better way to describe them. It was clinical and professional—though it did sound slightly cold. "The men who died. They worked there before."

"And you took these from there?" Emma's eyes were as wide as the huge cinnamon rolls she made in the early mornings.

"Yes," Katie admitted. "But I also came across something else." Her tone cued Emma to the fact that it wasn't a good thing she'd found.

"What? What did you find?"

"Is your *Daed* in any financial trouble?"

Emma looked confused by the question. "What does this have to do with anything?"

"Is he?" Katie pressed.

"No," Emma said frowning. "We are well off financially, not that it's any of your business." Her biting word shocked Katie.

"I didn't think—" Katie began.

"No, you didn't. How dare you come up to me and demand information when you won't even act like my friend. Our bakery is overrun with police and you sit here talking about our financial troubles as if you have the right to demand information."

Emma stood, snatching the seeds off the table. "I'll look these up, but only because my father's career is at stake. Not because you asked."

Then she turned and stormed into the library, where Katie knew she wouldn't be able to effectively apologize. Sighing, she rested her head against her hands. It was probably a good thing she hadn't mentioned that the police were there due to a clue *she* had given the detective.

The information Emma had shared did give Katie pause though. If Atlee Bender was in no need of finical help, why was his name on a list at the loan office?

Chapter 5

Katie walked along the road toward the guesthouse, her heart heavy. She was still excited about the case and the possibility of solving it, but her friend's anger toward her was understandable. Was she being unfeeling? She didn't think so—she was analytical, that was all—but maybe she hadn't shown enough compassion.

Her thoughts scattering in all directions, she almost didn't notice when the police car pulled up next to her. Nearly jumping, she looked to the side and saw Samuel in the front seat.

"Would you like a ride home?"

She considered this and shook her head no. She should keep her distance from the attractive detective. "No. But thank you. I'd prefer to walk."

Without saying anything, he sped ahead. Part of her felt disappointed that he'd gone, while the other part of her—the rational half—reminded her that it was a good thing. But why had he stopped in the first place?

Then she noticed that he'd pulled over to the side of the road where there was room for his vehicle. He climbed out and walked toward her. He'd left his suit coat in the car and, as he walked toward her, she noticed the way his shirt pulled across his shoulders. His forearms looked muscular as well, where his sleeves were rolled up from the cuffs to the elbow. She knew she shouldn't notice these things, but she couldn't help it.

She turned her gaze away to look out over the field when he approached. "Mind if I walk with you?"

She knew she should refuse, but she couldn't bring herself to. "No."

He fell into step with her and they walked toward the guesthouse.

"Why are you here?"

He was quiet for a while, and seemed to be taking in the surrounding area with deep breaths. "I wanted to see what you found out."

"What I—" she halted. Did he know she'd gone to the loan office? "What I found out *where*?"

Without looking at her, he continued, "Wherever it was that you and that *buwe* rushed off to."

She noticed his use of the word "boy" and nearly smiled. Was he jealous of David?

"We went to the loan office where Mr. Julander and Mr. Caldwater used to work. With them both gone, I thought that anyone left at the office could shed some light on the case."

"How did you know it was Jude Caldwater who'd died?"

"I didn't," she said, a little too smugly.

Samuel looked down at her, one eyebrow cocked. "Care to explain?"

"Simple deductive reasoning. Besides, I found out where Mr. Julander used to work and put the rest of the pieces together from what you'd said."

She caught the grimace that crossed his face. "I shouldn't have said anything."

"I haven't told anyone."

"*Denki*," he said, looking down at her.

His easy use of her language made her heart warm, and she blurted, "Do you miss it?"

He frowned. "Miss what?"

Had she really just asked him that? She was a foolish girl meddling in things she had no business in. "Your Amish roots."

"Oh," he said, looking away from her and off to the field again as if he could glean his answers there. "I do."

His words were a shock. She hadn't expected such an easy response. "Why did you leave in the first place?"

He rubbed a hand across his jaw, the stubble there causing a scratchy sound. "During my *Rumschpringe* I was befriended by a man who worked as a detective. He talked about his job and his love for it and I, always having loved a good mystery, thought it would be the perfect job. Unfortunately, there is no compromise between the *Englischer* world and ours with regards to police work."

She didn't miss the fact that he'd said "ours" when talking about the Amish world. Could it be that he still considered himself Amish? That wasn't possible though, of course.

"I sometimes think ..." he looked away again.

"What?" she prodded gently.

"I sometimes think I'll come back."

Gasping, she tried to calm the anxious pounding of her heart. He still hadn't come back. He still hadn't stepped away from a job he obviously loved doing.

They were near the guesthouse when Samuel stopped, causing her to take a few steps back to him.

"Katie, I just wanted to make sure you're being safe."

"I am," she said, his concern once again surprising her.

"Good." He looked up at the porch of the guesthouse and she followed his gaze. Emma was there, looking breathless. Had she run the whole way?

"I should go," he said, walking back the way he came.

Katie wanted to say something, but she had no words. Maybe, when the case was over, they could continue the conversation of him returning to the Amish community—even if that seemed like wishful thinking for Katie.

***

"You're sure spending a lot of time with the detective," Emma said when Katie joined her on the porch.

Katie felt the blush rush to her cheeks, and hoped Emma would think it was from the warmth of the day. "Nonsense. He was asking what I'd found, but there wasn't much to report."

"But he still wanted to know." Emma sent her a pointed look.

"Emma," Katie said, thinking about what she'd considered before. "I'm sorry."

Emma blinked. "Sorry?"

"Yes, for not being more understanding." Katie shook her head. "I've been most concerned about solving this case so that I can prove you and your *Daed* are innocent, but I may have done that and risked sounding cold or not understanding. That was never my intension. You are dear to me, my best friend, and I can't stand to think that someone would get away with framing you!"

"Oh!" Emma said.

"What?" Katie said, knowing the exclamation had nothing to do with what she'd just said.

"I just remembered why I was in such a hurry to get here."

Katie's pulse thundered in her ears. Emma had news about the case.

"What is it Emma?"

"Well first," she said, a smile transforming her features back into the warm, bubbly Emma that Katie knew so well, "thank you for you apology. I will admit that I was frustrated by your seeming lack of interest in how I was feeling and—"

"Emma, what did you find out?" Katie interrupted.

Her friend scowled at her, then nodded her head. "I suppose you're right. Apologies behind us, I was able to look through our records."

"How?" Katie interrupted again.

"Are you going to let me get this out or not?"

She rolled her eyes. "Continue."

"Thank you," Katie said. "I bring home our order book almost every day. Just to balance things at home and double-check. That way I know what I need to do the next day. So I looked through and came across the order for four blueberry muffins."

"The same muffin that killed our guest," Katie said, more for her own benefit. "But wait, did you say four?"

"Yes!" Emma's gaze was intense. "*Four.*"

That meant... "Does that mean there are two more muffins out there? Two more victims?"

Emma frowned. "Two? Don't you mean three?"

"Someone else died," Katie said, then immediately regret it.

"What!"

Emma demanded details that Katie didn't have. She also felt guilty because it didn't seem like news she was free to share, even though Samuel had shared it with her. She had a feeling he wasn't supposed to have said anything.

"It's a long story, but the important thing is that there are still two muffins unaccounted for."

"Yes, that, and I found something else." Emma swallowed hard.

"Tell me," Katie nearly demanded, the waiting almost too much for her.

"Those seeds you gave me were Hemlock seeds."

Katie knew the name but couldn't place it. "What does that mean?"

"Poison, Katie. That had to have been what killed those men!"

Chapter 6

Katie hardly got any sleep. She had wanted to go find a way to call Samuel, but her grandmother had insisted she clean the rooms for their new guests.

She'd realized that the police likely already knew about the poison. What they didn't know was the fact that there were more muffins. The only problem was that she didn't have any *hard* evidence. Yes, four muffins had been purchased and could be used as a means of poisoning someone else, but there was no guarantee that they would. Besides, the police were already doing all they could. She couldn't bother Samuel with her assumptions without something to give him.

She had told Emma to make sure that she and David were at the guesthouse in the early morning so they could discuss the case. When David showed up, Emma in the seat next him, she noticed the way they were laughing and joking with one another. It was odd, and yet Katie found she didn't mind. It made her happy to see David showing interest in Emma, but she vaguely wondered if she *should* care.

"*Gute mariye,* Katie," David said, helping Emma from the buggy.

She responded in kind and ushered them to the back porch where they could discuss things freely. Their new guests wouldn't come until early afternoon anyway, but Katie wanted to make sure they weren't disturbed.

"What is all of this about?" David asked.

"I need to talk out the details," she explained. "And you two can help."

Emma grinned, encouraging her, and she began to talk through the case. As she shared what she knew, she mentioned Philip Julander and Emma gasped.

"I know that name."

"How? From where?"

Emma frowned. "I remember my *Daed* saying something about him." She closed her eyes in thought. "Oh I know!" She brightened. "We, um, well; we got money from our *Grossdaadi* and *Grossmammi* when they died years ago. Apparently they were forced to sell their land and later it was discovered. They were given … I can't remember the word, but they were paid back the sum and much more."

"What does this have to do with Philip Julander?"

"You're impatient this morning," Emma said with a frown. "Because of this, my *Daed* likes to help out those who need money. Mr. Julander was a frequent patron at the bakery and *Daed* spoke with him about lending money once. I think it was to Eli Lapp, if I remember correctly."

It was Katie's turn to gasp. "I saw that name on the list!"

Her gaze connected with David's then shot to Emma's.

"What does it all mean?" she asked.

Katie frowned, thinking through the details. Why would Ralph have a list of names on his desk if—

"It wasn't his desk."

David and Emma looked at Katie bemused. "What?" they said in unison.

"At the loan office. Ralph wasn't sitting at his desk. Why else would there be a mug of coffee on his desk if he didn't drink it?"

David nodded. "That is strange. Do you think his desk was the one where you found those seeds?"

"I think so." She nodded slowly, wondering what this all meant.

"I think we need to talk to Sa—Detective Bradford," she said, barely catching herself. "He needs to know what we found."

They agreed and set off for town.

***

Samuel stood with his back to the perimeter tape at the bakery. She was surprised they still had it closed down, but it made sense since they still hadn't found the killer. Though she was beginning to have a good idea of who it was.

"Samuel?" she asked. She had asked David and Emma to give her a few minutes with the detective, and they seemed content to sit at the library down the street and wait for her. She was at once thrilled to speak with him alone, even as she warned herself to be cautious.

"Katie," he said, a smile transforming his usually stern face, "*Gute mariye.*"

"And to you," she said. Then she jumped into the explanation of what she'd found at the loan office, hoping that he could use some of the information she'd given him in some way.

"You are suspicious of Ralph Smithton?" He frowned. "I talked to him myself. He seemed very distraught, and there was nothing out of the ordinary. But I suppose I could talk to him again. But the Hemlock we already knew about. I'll keep that in mind though."

"And Eli Lapp," she felt a growing sense of dread in the pit of her stomach and rested her hand there. *Lord, are you trying to tell me something?*

"What about him?"

"I—I have a bad feeling." She flushed; knowing that detective work was about the hard facts, but she also knew the Lord played a large role in the pursuit of justice. She had to believe that He could guide her as much as her instincts and the clues could. "I think you should check on him. I know that you are busy and this is a terrible inconvenience but …" What else could she say?

"I trust you and your instincts Kate," he said, holding her gaze for a moment without saying anything. "I'll go check on him now."

"*Denki*," she said, some of the weight lifting.

"Will you be at the library later today?"

She nodded.

"Then I'll come tell you what I found there."

She watched as he climbed into his car and took off on a hunch that she had. She just hoped he would get there in time. For what, she wasn't sure, but she knew he needed to hurry.

———

Chapter 7

Katie saw Samuel's car before either Emma or David did, and suddenly felt nervous. She knew he was coming to talk to her—well, them—and had no idea what he would say. As he parked and climbed out of the car, David noticed him.

"Look who we have here," he said in a wry voice.

Katie shot him a look.

"Hello," Samuel said, approaching their table.

"What did you find?" Katie asked as soon as he was close enough.

"We found Eli Lapp at his house just in time."

Dread coursed through Katie. In time? "He was poisoned?"

Samuel nodded. "I think we got to him in time. But …" he glanced down at Emma, "I'm afraid there was evidence that your father had been there Emma. We need to bring him in for questioning."

"M-my father? That can't be! I'm sure he was at the bake—oh," she halted, realizing that he *couldn't* have been at the bakery. It was still closed by the police.

"I've sent agents to go to your house to retrieve him."

"Oh no," she said shaking her head. "He hadn't done anything. Why would he? He was going to *help* Eli."

Samuel glanced at Katie, then back at Emma. "I'm not sure, but I'll get to the bottom of this, I promise." He took a step back, nodding toward Katie. "I just wanted to let you know what I found out."

She wanted to follow him, to walk him to his car so they could talk in private, but she knew that it wouldn't look right in front of David and Emma. Instead she nodded at him and turned her attention back to her friends.

"This is terrible," Emma said, near tears.

"I'm sorry, Emma," David said. He looked distraught, more so than Katie had seen, and she wondered again at the connection between them.

"I—I need to go. I'll use my scooter to get home. My mother will need me there."

"Do you want us to go with you?" David asked.

"No, it'll be all right."

They watched as Emma nearly ran to her scooter and took off for home.

"Poor Emma," Katie said, turning to look at David, whose eyes were still following Emma down the path.

"Huh?" He said, turning back around.

"I feel bad for Emma."

"I do too. How can we help her?"

"By solving this case," Katie said decisively. She began to rehash everything they knew, all of the details and intricate things that may or may not be part of the solution.

"I would still say that Ralph has the most to gain."

"Why would you say that?"

"Well, if Atlee *is* lending Eli money, then that's one less loan that the bank could have received. Maybe Ralph knew that."

"But murder seems extreme, don't you think?"

"True," he nodded in agreement. "But some people will do awful things when money is involved."

Katie nodded, agreeing. Some people would.

***

Katie had woken up in the middle of the night with a revelation. It was one of the moments you have when you just *knew* the next thing to do, though you weren't completely sure how you'd gotten to that point.

It was now early in the morning, and she was on her way into town. She'd stopped by David's house, and he was able to borrow the buggy so they could pick up Emma and go to the police station.

Now, riding in the buggy in the early morning stillness, Emma asked, "What do you hope to find out, Katie?"

"I am going to ask if we can speak with your father, Emma. I know it's likely not allowed, but I'm going to hope and pray that *Herr Gott* will provide a way for us. I think he has answers to this whole thing that he may not even realize he knows."

"My father wouldn't hide anything from the police," Emma said, sounding hurt.

"No, I don't think that," Katie was quick to explain. "I think its pieces of the puzzle he doesn't realize he has."

When they arrived, they were shown to an office where Samuel sat behind a large desk strewn with papers. A bulletin board behind him had pictures of faces and papers tacked up all over it, and a window in the corner looked out over the parking lot, though it let in bright morning sunlight.

Samuel looked tired and a bit lost at the moment, but when his gaze caught Katie's he smiled. "What are you all doing here?"

"She forced us to come," David said with a laugh. He tried at humor, but it came out sounding forced.

"I was hoping we could all sit down and talk with Atlee. I know that that is probably not usually done, but you could be there. I think there are some questions that he can answer."

Samuel frowned. "We've already questioned him."

"I may ask questions you haven't," she offered.

Sighing, he stood and asked them to give him a moment. When he came back, he said they could have ten minutes with the man, though he'd have to sit in with them. They quickly agreed.

When Atlee was brought into the room, Emma jumped forward and gave him a hug before retreating back to the far corner where she would observe. She didn't want any part in the questioning, which Katie understood.

"Why are you here, Katie Zook?" he asked in a friendly tone.

"Because I think you may know more than what you've said."

"Katie!" Emma said from the corner.

She ignored her friend. "You know Mr. Julander, did you not?"

Atlee nodded. "I told the police this yesterday. I knew him."

"And did you two talk about money at all?"

"Well, yes, but loans. I wanted to know the best way to go about creating a loan for Eli Lapp, One that was fair and yet would show him the need to be responsible in paying it back."

"I thought so," Katie said triumphantly.

"What did he tell you?"

"Well," Atlee said, rubbing his beard in thought, "he gave me a plan that they were supposed to be using at the loan office."

"Supposed to?" Samuel broke in.

Atlee shrugged. "Philip had said that he'd come across something while at work that frustrated him, but he didn't share this with me. He only emphasized the need to be honest in my lending, which I had every intention of being."

"Of course," Katie said. Her gaze collided with Samuel's, and she hoped it conveyed that she needed to explain, but not in front of everyone.

"Katie, a word?" Samuel said.

She stepped out into the hall with him, happy that he had understood her perfectly.

"What is this about?"

"I think that Ralph Smithton was skimming money off of the loans he was giving out. Increasing their pay to the loan office, but not reporting it correctly. When Philip went to create a plan for Atlee for his loan, I think he came across figures that didn't add up."

Samuel started to say something, but frowned. "There's more, isn't there?"

Katie grinned; he really was beginning to understand her. "Yes."

"My *Grossmammi* said that Mr. Julander had come to our guesthouse for quiet time to think. I *think* that he was deciding how he would approach Ralph about what he was doing."

"But where does Eli come in to all of this? And Jude?"

"I don't have all of the answers, but I think that Jude must have found out, possibly from Philip. I believe it was Ralph's intention to frame Atlee though."

"That would make sense. We found a hat belonging to him on the front porch. But Eli said that Atlee was never there. It was just left to draw suspicion to him."

"Where is Ralph now?" she asked.

Samuel's face grew dark. "I don't know. When I went to talk with him yesterday, he wasn't at home or his office."

"Could he have fled?"

"It's possible." Samuel looked at his watch. "I've got an idea, but I need to go now."

"All right," she said. He turned to go, but stopped. "Good work, Katie."

She smiled, watching his tall form disappear down the hall. If anyone could find and stop Ralph Smithton, it was Detective Samuel Bradford.

Chapter 8

Katie and David sat outside of the library, waiting. It was their usually day to meet with Emma, but since the bakery was still closed they weren't sure if she would come—or *could* come. They'd had no word on Ralph Smithton, or any of the mystery since they had left the police station the day before.

"Do you think he was able to find that Ralph fellow?" David asked.

"I hope so. I would assume it depends on where he disappeared to."

David nodded slowly. "Do you think Emma is coming?"

Katie assessed David's longing, far-off look. "Do you fancy her?"

His attention jerked in her direction. "F-fancy her?" His cheeks turned pink. "I-I don't know what you mean."

She had her answer. "So you do."

He looked uncomfortable.

"It's all right if you do," Katie said, wanting to make him feel at ease. "She's my best friend and you're also my friend. I would be so happy to see you two together. Will you ask to drive her home after the next frolic?"

His shoulders relaxed. "Do you think I should? I mean, will she say yes?"

"I think she would," Katie said with a smile.

He nodded. "Then I think I will."

Katie was about to respond when Emma came into sight, riding her kick scooter. She looked happier than she had yesterday, and Katie wondered if that meant good news.

"He's home," Emma said, breathless from her ride. "My *Daed,* he came home this morning. A nice policeman dropped him off. I'm so relieved."

"What happened? Did they tell him why they were letting him go?"

Emma opened her mouth to reply but stopped.

"Emma—" Katie started, exasperated.

But Emma held up a finger, pointing. Turning around, Katie saw Samuel coming toward them from the direction of the bakery.

"Samuel," she said, not thinking about the fact that she'd used his first name in front of her friends.

"Hello everyone," he said, nodding at David and Emma then turning back to Katie. "I suppose you heard the good news."

"Well, part of it. We just know that Emma's father is back. I'm curious about the rest though!"

"Of course you are," he said with an easy smile. "Let's sit."

As they did, he began to explain. "I put out an alert on Ralph's vehicle, and he was pulled over just before he crossed state lines. It was close. When we brought him in, I had a little chat with him." Samuel smiled a cunning smile. "I had evidence that he'd purchased the hemlock seeds, and presented this to him along with your theory, Katie. He looked like I just told him his own plan, then he admitted to everything."

"I was right?" Katie asked.

"Spot on." Samuel held her gaze for longer than necessary before continuing his explanation. "He *had* been skimming money off the top, and when Philip found out about it he felt he had no choice but to kill him. Apparently he has a background in plant biology, and knew about hemlock's poisonous affects. The idea to use the bakery came when he made the connection between Eli and your father, Emma. He wanted to frame Atlee for Philip's murder and be done with it, but then Jude came into the picture. He figured if he killed one more person, it would lead suspicion away from him."

"He was very wrong."

"Indeed." Samuel looked down at his clasped fingers. "I'm glad that you all were able to help. The information you gave me was invaluable. I can't thank you all enough."

They all shook their heads in modesty.

"I've got to be going, though." He stood, his gaze lingering again on Katie.

"I'll walk you to your car," she said, standing. He looked relieved, like he'd been saved from asking her to come.

As they walked, Katie looked up at him, trying to guess what he wanted to say, if anything, to her.

"Katie," he finally said, "I didn't want to say anything in front of them, but I got in trouble for sharing information with you."

She gasped. "I'm so sorry."

"It's not your fault," he said quickly, "I didn't tell you to make you feel bad, only so that you would know. I may be sent on temporary leave. I'm not sure what their disciplinary action will be. But I may not be here if …" he trailed off.

Her stomach warmed at his words. He was worried about her should something else happen in Summervale.

"I'll miss you," she said, then regretted her words immediately. He was no longer Amish, it wasn't right for her to think about him as she was. But she couldn't help how she was drawn to him.

He stopped, frowning down at her. "If I wasn't a detective …"

She desperately wanted him to finish his sentence so she could know what he was going to say, but he clamped his mouth shut.

"You know," she said, regaining her humor and wry smile, "I do an awful lot of detecting for an Amish woman."

He laughed, allowing her humor to loosen him. "I suppose you do."

They stayed there for a moment, looking into one another eyes, and then he stepped back toward his car. "Don't go getting yourself in trouble, do you hear?"

"No sir," she said with another smile. "I shall be the most careful sleuth possible."

"Good." He looked at her for another moment, then got in and drove off. She stood there, outside the bakery that was no longer swarming with police, and watched him drive away.

What did God have in store for them—if anything? Would she see Samuel again? What would happen to him because of him sharing information with her? They had solved the case; shouldn't his superiors be happy about that?

She sighed and turned back toward David and Emma. She was happy for them. More than that, she was happy that the case was solved and that a murderer had been placed in jail.

If only things had ended on a happier note for Samuel. Before joining her friends, her last thought was more of a prayer.

God, bring Samuel home.

∗∗The End∗∗

Please Check Out My Other Books

Murder in Amish County

The Amish Casket Case

The Amish Animal Detective

The Amish Muffin Murder

Thank You

Many thanks for taking the time to buy and read through this book.

Hope you enjoyed the book; please take a moment to leave your honest review.

With Regards,

Ruth Bawell

Made in the USA
Lexington, KY
15 July 2016